33 Crystal Skulls
& The Anti+Christ

BOOK 2 OF 7

33 Crystal Skulls & The Anti+Christ
UNCENSORED, UNEDITED, RETRACTED INVENTION VERSION

GOD'S WORDS ARE IN OUR HUMAN CODE

1ST EDITION MANUSCRIPT Paper/Hard cover

E-BOOK   978-1-967897-02-5
PAPERBACK   978-1-967897-12-4
HARDCOVER

33 Crystal Skulls & The Anti+Christ
Chapter 2, PART 2 OF 7
by RAPHAEL / Rafael G.

Dedicated to

GOD

In God we trust.
Our true spark of, cosmic static, spiral core of all our inner sparks, ghosts / spirits. Whatever the force within us, is called.

God is perpetually awesome.
Thank you God for everything.
Please forgive our iniquities. 1971-2

The Human breath of life. An internal, Autonomous program, for humans, extra sensory boost of pure life. An App/program defibrillator life support, for emergencies, for Humans.

CHAPTER TWO

Moonbase 33

978-1-967897-12-4

Moon base 33

The Lost Souls of

The End

The year is December 2666.

Michael is introduced:

"Good Evening, this is Michael
Angelo on VxO-XoXio..O news at 12:00.

Grab your emergency supplies, get
your families, hurry up, and hide from the
liquid raindrops of Hell, if you can.

Today we are sadly reporting the end of the world appears to be finally occurring, and now the end has been bestowed upon the planet. As many stories of history, and prophecies have warned us in the past to prepare, and pray for this day to never occur. Nothing physically or mentally can really prepare us or yourself for this day. As harsh as that may sound. The fact of the matter is the end has been bestowed upon us all."

Michael turns his head with a smirk on his face, and says;

"Well most of us at least. The truth of the matter is the end of the world is a day of great sadness for all. Well most of us at least."

As Michael adjusts his tie, pulls out a cigar on Live Exact Air Digital Waves, and then puts a freaky smile on his face, throwing away his notes, and key cards in the air.

Camera man Bob looks at Michael, and says.

"The F1150 Space Rover did blow up, so you do remember Michael you are still live on IviewerTV? We do not have to go to commercial till these tragedies blow over. So Mericanas out there listen up, to Michael as he bestows upon you a new meaning of what a real venture of time of lost and forgotten history. The true stories of scriptures, what is known, as The Lost Souls."

Michael rolls his eyes, smirks a bit and continues:

"Practically all prophesies of history, and some fake, fly by night prophet pastors have been false, and wrong with predictions, of the end of the world."

=={As, Michael stares into the camera eyes of trans-viewers, and grimly says, with a smirk.}

"Unfortunately, today is now beyond time to prepare or estimate when the end is, since this day is now among our planet. These current drastic events are presently occurring in most regions of the planet. So far the most horrific hour of humanity has ever faced is today.

Scientific theories have assumed that mysteriously, somehow, someone or something has molecularity sent a projectile laser beam, to, and from the sun, and back to your planet.

According to scientific statistical studies, this projectile laser beam has transmitted a very high power frequency to, and from certain regions of this planet. These sun flares have been considered to be similar to what is considered a huge solar flare R.F. transmission signal.

This strategic laser beam has created a molecular gamma disruption in the H_2O structure of the ocean water. Thus, changing

of the hydrogen molecular structure of the
H2O salt water, and igniting like charcoal
fluid for BB-Q's. This in turn has made
water fire that is blasting the salt waters,
making it a strategic hydrogen bomb. The
planet is now looking, and becoming a
hydrogen sulfuric sea lake of fire in some
parts of the world."

Michael smiles nodes his head looks
down, and then up, and continues.

"You may call these tragedies the
covenant wrath from God, Armageddon, the
rapture, the end of the world, higher power
chaos, the unforgiving grim reaper. Satan at
work, winning the war, or whatever you may
want to call, the wrath, of these horrific
events. Fate has now finally been vested,
and arrived upon us, on our little planet.

Not later, but, the day is today. The big worm hole tornado that sucks us in different solar nations up above has been temporarily out of service for a few centuries now. As if the Devil finally got a hold of the God device, and used the hydrogen laser projectile bomb, instead of uniting man kind. Go figure.

As recorded classical history has taught us that similar repetitive prophecies, in our history books, are the infamous calendars, that end with a mystery that does not share its buried past. Some humans viewing or listening, know what I am referring to in these ancient hieroglyphs, that the greedy ones, might posses. Our ancestral civilizations from our history have predicted stories that are similar with the same ending cycles of repetitive astrology alignments. All end, with a mystery ending.

These stories are similar as the speculated Mayans prediction of the infamous date of, December 21, 2012. Chiena landed in Americana long before Americana did, and took a copy of the Mayan calendar back to Chiena with the story spreading, and then extinguishing out like most legends of Warnings from time, and war.

Even when Americanas' uncovered the continent, the Made in Chiena signs were all around the parts of the continent. These special markers, which were left behind, were big donut anchors left in the ocean coastlines. Many other artifacts were left behind in ruins from tsunami waves, and killing almost all of the travelers.

Evidence of other artifacts left were from the immigrants from Southern lands that traveled to the North regions. They traveled from underground ancient caves from Mayan territories to survive the unjust slays from the South.

These tribes of Mayan villagers migrated North to warn their families in Northern regions, and they costumed themselves, disguising themselves with a look of different tribes to hide from slaughters from the foreigners that invaded the peaceful villages in the South. For falsely saying the decapitations were for the name of God.

The migrants hid from punishment of death for their religious beliefs. The sword came from certain religious blasphemers, which were, greater sinners from across the oceans. The foreign criminal trespassers, intentionally scribed that they killed because of misunderstood classical law customs of blasphemy. The invaders didn't understand the culture and customs of what they thought were sacrifices to innocent villagers, were not.

When in fact the sacrifices were actually, suicidal humans, and criminal Mayans that were really in fact getting the death penalty from their crimes, or wishes. That is why these criminals were painted blue. Back then criminals did not wear orange jump suits but, permanent blue paint to tell everyone they are intended for criminal sacrifice. These criminals were judged, and then sentenced to the death penalty by punishment of sacrifice.

This civil community used blue full body paint to identify criminals, or suicidal members, and were permanently marked by being painted blue. This showed others in their civilization that these humans were criminals or might be dangerous, and deserved the death penalties to be given to them. They could never hide as they were marked for life. The criminals were rightfully judged, and were to be executed for felony crimes, as contemporary society accepts the death penalties for certain crimes.

These humans were not only the best governed communities on the planet that believed in the death penalty. The criminals were also sacrifices to be put inside deep liquid wells, deep within the planet and their blood to feed the planet with minerals, and vitamins from the corpse. This was believed to percolate, and vein in the planet to make the soils rich for harvest. For the circle of life, is the circle of life. As a worm makes composite from rubbish of vegetation, to give nutrients, to the circle of life.

These wells located in specific parts of the planet were believed to be an artery for the planet that would feed off, the human flesh sacrifices, and nourish the lands with microorganism distributing into water.

Allowing distribution to many regions of crops, to fruition and nourishment. Continuing the nourishment of the circle of life, within the planets veins.

But the foreign invaders that went to the Mayan communities, true plan was that they wanted all the gold, not, knowledge.

The trespassers wanted to take the riches of an advanced community with burdensome laws, from a rich peaceful culture, that would unknowingly render the planets future radiation shield. Nothing mattered to these greedy Devils, whom claimed they were men with God. The surviving Mayans, scattered, and migrated in many numbers to safer known established regions across the lands. For many years, and they disguised themselves with different

tribal Indian looks, and steered away from
their original origins, to hide, from the
religious blaspheming, which cursed
themselves, from their traditions, of not
following God.

The invaders true greed was for they
sought gold, and not the true use of the
religions power for good. The foreigners
were tempted by the Devil himself, the very
snake from the Garden of Edem was present
that day of the massacres. The snake
persuaded Diego to kill, and take the gold
as it was rightfully his, and should never
belong to a community that believed in
killing blue-covered men, as sacrifices to a
God they didn't understand.

The foreigners' invasion on the land
was unjust and abuse of the death penalty

for greed of gold, and not for justice.
Important documents were lost and
destruction for the Mayan communities. The
Mayans ran for safety as their lives would
be in jeopardy for many centuries to come,
from the South, and the greed from the
trespassers from the North. As the Galaxy
was in a part of the Universe, which is
strong in Evil induction waves.

Many original woven, books of the
very evolved peaceful community of the
Mayans were lost forever. The Mayans for
centuries were about peace, and progression.

As all the Northern, and Southern
lands were conquered by the Mayans, by
peaceful methods, and growing from
progression from the instructions from The
Crystal Skull plans. The present would be

different in flying, and transporting
technology for around the world, and be a
one united community.

The Mayans were not prepared for
fighting in the masses like what was brought
to them from the foreigners. Their wars were
over. Since their peaceful, gullible,
leaders, were dead. They had peace in the
lands for centuries. The Mayans ran to warn
the families in the Northern, and Southern
nations. The Mayans had to be in disguises,
with different outfits, as to disguise
themselves as different tribes so their
children would not be slaughtered by the
unjust blaspheming liars, that came for the
land, and gold to hoard. Their mission was
to hide all the pyramids on the planet under
ground, so they would not be found. Until

recently, we believe we have finally found all of them.

The stories of all that occurred were passed on by generations, misfits in folk tales, and then laughed upon as customs changed, and a new poor system, and corrupt government emerged. All true customs would be lost and buried as the temples were buried so the portals could not be found by the invaders, and all was lost for centuries to come. The greedy people are what caused the wrong outcome, and even their own extinction from the higher power. As the inevitable became the results. So the planet was programmed to be tipped, to hide, and bury the planets treasures, with mountains, and water.

Some concluded the Mayan calendar, and many other prophecies predicted when the world would finally come to an end being similar with mystery conclusions. Even other super natural prophecies of the past and stories have predicted the end times, about the future being annihilated, and all human life on our planet demised. It's a saddened end time. But all have been wrong. The Mayan calendar historically uses a 18-Month, annual calendar year, and thus the grand prediction of fatalities, to occur or that the world would conclude its ending at 2012 was way off, and wrong.

Long ago one very sharp archaeologist translated the predictions correctly, that many great known famous visitors from the stars above would be appearing December 21, 2012.

The alignment for great mass to travel, and leap a billion light years away by the galaxy's natural light alignment of the stars, would allow great masses to travel that particular day, and be returning from Olivia's asteroid belt.

December 21, 2012, was the day, these great tribes would meet again. Bringing cities of people to unite, with distant families, that worked the land, to prepare the great day, of the biggest celebration, known to this planet.

All the pyramids would have been completed, and space travel of large cities would have been transported into, what is called the Gulf of Mexico. The shape was there to put more cities, and divert all tornadoes, and destruction from hurricanes. Transporting land, and filling the Gulf with land mass from the transportation of the Great pyramids, technological power. Where other Great hidden pyramids, are currently, situated all over the planet."

Michael takes a drink of water, and continues to say.

"We will be right back, after this announcement, from our sponsors."

A commercial is heard, and the singing begins by saying.

"Mega Megatastic, cola is so yummy, yummy sola, cola yummy yummy cola is caffeine cola, yummy yummy cola, drink it everyday, yummy yummy. Go, and power up, and buy my yummy yummy Mammi for my tummy, yummy yummy, for my tummy, yummy yummy, Mega, Mega, Mega, Mega, Mega, cola, Mega, Mega, Mega, Yummy, Megatastic colaaaaaaaa."

"I know we do not have sponsors anymore, but I just like that song. I guess it would not hurt now to disclose some Top Secret information that has been kept a secret for a few Thousand years. There is no more reason to, not disclose this information to the viewers now."

==Michael looks very excited, and rubs his hands together, then nods his head and says.

" It is now finally time to disclose the naked truths of the past. I am willing, and now can disclose this mesmerizing information without fearing death from my peers. The reason why I am disclosing this is that since recently exactly five hours ago, and then recently, checked, and confirmed five more times, a total of 10 times verified. It is now officially confirmed, to all our audiences, that our current President, Head of state, the main bosses, producers, designers, and some creators of the space shuttle Model 0004 have been hit by sand blasting particles from, moon fragmented asteroids hurling in space."

===Michael looks to the floor, and shuts his eyes for a minute. Then changes the frequency stations, to live, on D.A.W..

(Digital Air Waves Inc.)

And Michael then with a straight face says.

"Thank you, for this, quite moment, we all shared, here live, on VOXKIL 101 D.A.W.."
I can call it anything I want as I am Michael, and I am now the boss!

Then with a devilish look Michael says "DAAAAAAAA. Don't you know? We can call this broadcasting, streaming powerhouses, anything we now want."

Michael then with a silly face says.

"The highlight of the hour is that supposedly, an over rated, over hyped, highlighted bomb proof space craft that your tax dollars paid for, did not save the lives of the most important passengers from this world, or God's anger.

The ones that were going to repopulate the planet after all other life was deceasing.

Officially confirmed, that all the futures re-Populating, big wigs for this planet, are dead. The V.I.P. passengers aboard the ship are all confirmed as fatalities."

Michael then with a smiling face says.

" I can hear the elite on that ship proclaiming and saying God is not our protector. He did not save us from the planet destruction. We built this space ship, and us the elite will survive, and conquer the planet once more after it is destroyed. We the elite, will live forever. And now, they're dead.

This in fact, was not, a Noah's ark ending, for the dead VIP ship, for sure.

These tragedies killed more than 100,000 humans aboard the stock holder's space craft, killing every passenger, and live stocks inside the ship. Including THEE, head honchos, that would have ordered our termination if I released what I am about to streamline on the network, and what I am going to be disclosing to all our trans-viewers this evening. "

{Michael, adjusts his tie straight.}

Clears his throat and continues:

"What I am going to share with you is
a very top secret. But I will tell you
anyway. This forced voyage to other sectors
around the universe, is known as (Time
Interchange Converting) or, also known as,
(TIC).

That is what prompted the decision
that was executed down to the recent last
protocol, which would be decided by the
leaders of the world.

All the leaders took off in the
trillion-dollar space shuttle trying to
reach a nearby TIC hole. The only space
shuttle that took off before getting hit by

moon fragments was a drone, and passages safely.

But the other ships received large fragmented rocks, and ashes that intertwine with the massive intake whirlwind engines, due to the solar shields being inoperable from all the fragmented meteoroids hitting them."

===Michael, drinks more water, and continues:

"All current, survivors, that are tuned in, are tuned in, and will be induced, to an all around, current frequency adjustment to the Emergency Broadcast tuners frequency. It is a state, and union coded world transmission broad casted, and only used as a now DE-facto analog coded union

transmission to all the remote-viewers tuned
in.

This is what one pilot announced over
the airwaves live, a few minutes ago."

"We are under attack by controlled
meteoroid fragmented projectiles, and large
dust that is clouding up the skies. We
believe they are coming from a magnetic
meteoroid belt near our galaxy. These were
signs of the times, and then shown by the
last sign."

The radio muzzles, and complete
static is now heard.

===Michael rolls his eyes.

"All that were chosen for this mission on the surviving planet are now burning souls, and the chosen Moon crowd colonies are not doing any better. All of them have been annihilated, and then their surviving souls will be transported to one of the official covenanted Grapevines.

This is where good, and bad souls get put high above the heavens before they get judged. We broke the soul or ghost dilemma theories from <u>The Angelic, Book of The Demised</u>, more than a century ago. A technology cracked, about 150 years ago, from Mayan hieroglyphs, and that is why we have top news, so quickly.

The visions are only visible through a worm hole algorithm, that is, a parallel world viewer. There are only three in

existence that we know of. The FBI has two
of them.

These current events are happening on
the planet as we speak, with fires, and
burning lava on the planet, killing the
masses. The whole atmosphere seems to be
burning. In fact some areas have reported as
50 feet of lava, and mass air inhalation
hazards from lava fumes.

These next images will bring a nasty
feeling, knowing your alive, and those
events are not happening to you. The proof
is that the present events around the world,
are causing communication problems, and
outages all around the world.

These events are once in a lifetime,
and an end, to some cultures, and nations.

This of course is what will be, and is in place of your contemporary normal life that you are, presently in. And is something yet to be seen, if any human survives these tragedies that many feared, would occur one day.

Well, today is that day. Wait no more. No more suspense on how it is going to end. The day is here, ironically 06:06:`06 AM., are when these events started. A complete paradox, the day and time, it started."

Michael continues to take the show, and anchor out his co-workers from his non scripted opinions of his own extraordinary way of talking, and his words were angelic in his opinion of the higher power.

"As some would say."

"What the practicality of current Classical Title Law will bring to humanity is unity, as a whole."

Michael, continues with that weird look in his eyes.

The assignment and bet were simple. The recorder for the main man above, assigned a deed to the manipulating, real deal con, Daddy of all Daddies. Lucifer P. Devilonianoplague. After a mutual, secret bet, Lucifer proposed an offer to God.

God agreed as his mysterious ways, are his, for allowing the challenge to occur. Angels loving God agreed, and trusted in him. God did once again test the people as he once did with Jobe. Those that passed the test went to the next realm as so did the ones that failed. Different realms were agreeing, on the bet, but few knew what would be the outcome.

After time passed, the trials were finally done, and from the past, crimes against humanity, God set the Devils fate. The Devils, and Demons were charged with many crimes as, influencing events to occur against Gods favor. So God gave a revocable lease of the planet to the Landlord Lucifer. To test all Angels, and to see their fates come forward.

We control our destinies, and choices for life. But, the planet you're on is where the test is. Morals determine your judgment. Until God assigns the world back to humanity from his great covenant, title will be held by the Devils. Mother Planet was saddened by the new lease, as plants withered all around the Universe. But yet the strong Angels in faith survived, and will survive, once more with the tests that brings, results of past chosen paths. That will bring what sows, ye will then, reap."

Michael laughs a bit and continues.

"However, long ago, when the world was leased, to the evil infamous Arch Angel, by the name of many names. The Grandfather Devil himself knew he wanted to become the permanent owner of all of God's glories. As the Devil, had to have an army to battle for the heavens, and worlds, he was planning to put under sulfuric acids, to burn the people that loved God.

Disguised as his real form, an Angel throughout eternity, tricking simple-minded humans, to believe, and pray to false idols, like statues, and crosses, or names of Saints that had no powers to do what God can do.

To do against The Ten Commandments, and do against the true written manuscripts that were downloaded into humans since the beginning of time. The Devil created his own church, and built many all over the world putting false idol of Gods, to infuriate the one, and only true God.

Lucifer infiltrated the true churches of God, and made many pseudo saints by diverting them to evil. Some of the saints were empowered by his visions for decades.

The robes, the saints wore were not questioned, and some fake men infiltrated the churches without proper credentials of being true men of the higher power. When in fact were the biggest sinners to this day.

God forgave some of the saints, since they were doing the scripture, written for them of fate. Like a parasite, attached to its host. We can proceed with our own choices but are scheduled to do what was on the plan that was written for each one of us. They are check points in life, and once you cross the border, than you are given choices. Then you proceed again, with more check points of life.

May it be to be, somewhere at a certain time, and you are destined to the checkpoint?

Whatever, it may be at the time of the check point. An assignment for what you ask? May it be to upload your daily events from your brain, to the hard drive clouds, up above? Uploading, and downloading instructions, choices, and life events that no matter what, somehow you were destined to be at this or that spot right now.

You're in a Checkpoint. No one can get out of doing a check point, (like sleep), etc.. You are supposed to be here reading this for part of the next time you upload this information to the Static Systemic Cloud above. Your assignment in the cloud, while you sleep is to ask God for forgiveness for every good soul.

Once you sleep, and you wake up, you are given another Checkpoint. A new chance, in life. You are awake, and breathing with us, brothers, and sisters. May we see each other, or never see each other but believe we have walked on this planet as a witness, recording data, and uploading, to the big server above.

If you do not believe, than evil is what comes out. The Devil will help you negatively, if you do not believe in him. He will infiltrate your space, and give you decisions where they will benefit the Devil only.

We are screwed if you get influenced by them. So BEWARE.

Your next upload, will bring Karma into your life. Wake up. There were, and are, those humans whom, he did not forgive, and are dead. Since God gave you a choice, all your life, and he patiently waits, for you, lurking to the day he allows you to be in line for your sentence to be.

For some there is a design made for certain choices, but are allowed few choices from the design. Some shoes were designed for you before you even knew you were going to buy them. The design was made for whatever God allowed us to contribute into this present state we are in. But with choices, from the design of life, that God created."

Michael continues with wide, eyes opened, and, almost dazing into his own spoken words. His mind was distracted, realizing that many viewers would be tuning on or reading his show for the last time.

As Michael continues for the next few minutes, feeling light headed in the brain from the cigar he was smoking.

His words felt empty to him like nothingness, and meaningless, since he knew God was taking the final judgment day into effect.

He closed his eyes again, morning a bit to the already dead humans, that were transmitted by cameras, through satellites. Other cameras were, also, recording, and displaying, the terror occurring around the world. As Michael slurred words, watching the horror occurring all over the world. He begins to cry, and then stops after seven seconds. He inhales deeply, and with a positive look in his eyes, says:

"We hope everyone listening will be able to join us after this huge planet cools in 48 hours."

Then Michael realizes, with a weird, scared look in his eyes. That many peoples, souls, their inhalation, and exhalation of cool coded Ox will not be passing into their lungs. The fresh airs, with the pleasure, of cool oxygen of life. He thinks to himself that some humans would have the right, to be here unless the all mighty one pulls the permanent plug.

The videos showed many humans praying, and yelling, and crying for their lost loved ones. It seemed like a plague of so much disaster, the true ending of one last, exhalation of the really true cool breath of life. The second, at birth, the breath of life was given to us by God, was the start of life. But now, the oxygen had finally seized, to an end, for many."

Michael continues:

"The life of, induction through the neurotic, and ionic field is now disrupted for millions of humans that were in the one network connection we call life. With all of us looking out, through the window of what we call our eyes, seeing our hands, tips of

our noses, and bodies. Wondering, what else
is there?

Knowing for many, they will soon find
out. Not by the false teachings of the past,
but knowing death, as a reality, to the
unfortunate ones, that were melted back to
the planet's elixir. Realizing that all,
preparations were useless to the disaster
that occurred, to the curses that were
covenanted, by the final actions."

Michael burps from his high
protein lunch, and continues:

"Well here goes, I will now tell you
about many close case studies, and new
technologies used to analyze the recently
discovered relics around the world. A few
years ago, a team on a quest to find the

relics, discovered in the Jungles of Mexico,
a map to The Crystal Skulls.

These well, known discoveries, are a
well-known archaeologist's dreams from
(THIS) Technological Historical Integrated
Systems. An artistic form of technology,
discovery exploding from downloads, from
Crystal Backup drives displayed in last
months, ATHIS magazines."

"This Scientist, who was a busy body
had recently made a new break through
discovery, on the relics found in an
underground pyramid cave in Mexico. Under a
well preserved well. Hidden, in an
underground, temple.

Some say that, this was the Holy
Grail of relics.

As actually prove-en, and corrected, by historians. They have confirmed that the Mayan calendar did confirm some major events, which did occur, along time ago in 2012.

Sadly, hardly anyone that mattered on the planet knew about it. Until an App that was called, 33 Crystal Skull Unity Map. It was downloaded on every device, to vote, on the spot. It would give G.P.S. coordinates, to the Crystals, and there was no way of tricking the system, as each voting device, knew where you were, your blood pressure, and diagnostics for living humans. This technology saved lives, and allowed a voting system for the people. The robots did everything for humans. By working together changed the world. But instead, crooked

Devil men, made the current world events occur. What do you think would happen when you changed the planets masses around?

The Mayan Calendars were not predictions of the world ending as people were led to believe but a time clock of when a portal of a giant algorithm, a black hole dimension, on the opposite side of the Moon would return a civilization of families.

There are days that if you go out and look at the Moon, it has a huge looking ring around it. The ring is from our Nova Sun. But some cool days, there are, really large hole images, behind the Moon. It is a giant planet, near the planet, you reside on. But you cannot see it unless you were taught where, and when to look for in the sky. This is not something you learn at any school.

Satellites do not point that direction for some reason, those days either. Weird, right? Some would say it's the sunlight reflecting a circular ring. But certain, astrological calendar years it is written that a planet window opens, for planet jumps.

Unfortunately, this technology was never completed, as scheduled by the leaders of the union. It would have opened a portal to another galaxy across the universe, allowing mass transportation. The portal would have allowed current habit-ants on this planet to travel to, and from the planet. Califas would have, electrocuted safely back to another planet, the way a lightning bolt, strikes.

With, and when all the transportation
equipment was functioning, and in tact,
would function correctly. The four D
machines printed on the fabric of elements,
and ions, molecularity creating the chosen
patterns of human choices.

Some believe these great inventions
of technology came from other planets. Other
Scientists have said the artifacts were
built and left by a highly evolved race.
Some concluded that, our ancient ancestors
that resided on this planet for uncountable
years, may have built it.

Before God, destroyed the planet six
times, the inventions of destruction, were
buried, and found again. We are on number 7
planet destruction, by the way if your

wondering. And have unfortunately, already
lost the Prius elite children.

It is just our listening or viewing
audience hearing our words. We are still
alive, and hope you are as well as can be.
Will humans make God, extinguish, all life,
as we know it again?

The old technology, which was
discovered, came with instructions. To
create peace, and safety, for the abiding
citizens, and to strategically place, 12
leaders, in charge on certain regions of the
planets' radius. They were to build, these
alien devices, that would cause, a cut into
the magnetic field.

This will allow long distance travel,
or would have allowed this phenomenon of

calculated, encrypted algorithms for land, travel, and much more amazing things to be possible.

This in fact would allow the phenomena of mass space travel for the occupants on this beautiful planet. This great and advance portal would not work or be visible on foot from the planet. But visible, only standing on a certain spot, on the Moon.

If you were on the Moon, and found the 12 pyramids on the Moon inside the craters you would find that, the pyramids were also strategically placed. The pyramids were made to complete the circuit of the advanced technology that could be used to transport these large masses of city, and land.

This advance technology consists of beacons integrated software into golden looking art tablets being the hardware. Certain precise cut gems, and super advanced, hard-core encrypted software integrated into the golden masses of conducting transmitters were used. This would sync mass ionic manipulation.

One part of the circuit dismantled would make the system not function properly without all the pillars or pyramids in tact and strategically placed on the planet and the Moon.

Also, certain types of stones were needed as giant semi conductors, and other elements being circled, and shaped with massive stones in their proper places. This would be as a motherboard or what you would call a computer. Of course other golden inducing hardware, had to be in its strategic place, on the planet and aligned with the Moon. For the giant advanced system to work.

Without the knowledge of the Planetarium hardware, the general public would not be able to see the black hole opening on the other side of the Moon.

No one would know, that there would be a large city on the other side of the Moon hiding the secrets of extra terrestrial beings. Alien to us, but human in nature, would in fact be able to exist adjacently to us. Living as a large, hidden city, on the other side of the Moon, that humans would never know about or see.

The Moon, being our neighbor, and the other hidden side of the Moon not being visible holds a mystery. Half of the Moon is mostly blinded to our eyes. As this hidden technology could transport a huge city for attacks, but normally this advanced technology, is known, by only peaceful civilizations. Normally only they have been able to puzzle, and crack the code.

This technology was made for the mind of peaceful cultures, and evil minds would never be able to crack such an advance technology. As it was triggered for destruction, from evil minds.

If one of the strategically placed tablets or Crystal Skulls on the pillars or pyramids were not completed, or the system was taken out of place on purpose, would render it dangerously useless. Then only a slight transmission, of the aliens, from different channels or dimensions would be able to transmit, certain limited signals. The system could be manifested by evil doers if the system was not completely built, with the firewall on. Similar to a computer, running, without an active firewall.

Hackers could channel into the planet code, with their firewall being off, if the system was not completed. The signal unfortunately could come from, all over. Good or bad signals may be intercepted. As the Devilions evil used the good of humans to crack part of the code.

On record there were a few signals that got transmitted into our historical record archives. To our knowledge there were signals transmitted, and recorded on YouTube.com. As we had traced the signal, and sent out a message on December 21, 2012. It is still on line, up from our knowledge, as the message is really, confusing at first.

The signal that did come from a suspected dimension was recorded the day the Mayan calendar predicted the channel would open up. Which was on December 21, 2012. The day was near, when, the big celebration for two worlds, with a great plan, of an advanced peaceful world would meet again. Bringing, culture, and knowledge to this great technology, for your planet.

Since the path way to the black hole is obstructed, by the Moon, not many would

ever know there is life on the Moon.
However, It is where some of us humans, now
live.

As of December 21st there was a
signal that came through to one of the
registered golden tablets. That supposedly
has not been discovered, and is still
secretly buried, somewhere in the planet.
The transmission was short, but was recorded
on Youtube.com. As correctly predicted from
the newly discovered tablet.

On December 21, 2012, as the Mayans
predicted, their human sibling, and
companions would have arrived, and
transported more land masses to our planet.
They would be the ones that would be putting
a wall to not let trespassers, like Columbus
and others did in the past.

However, with the system taken off-line, none of this was possible. If you were to look at the Mayan calendar, you would notice a man looking through the worm hole peeking with a smile.

He is also known as Mikotepachio. A great joker, and a good leader, of the tribe. He was sticking his tongue out, as he loved, drinking, his no caffeine, coffee. He was wiping his lips from that delicious brew he loved.

The tribe would always have a batch for him made by the hundreds of gallons stored on Coffee Planet 2. He labeled his yummy coffee as Mikotepachio Mocha Chip Café.

The calendar shares the distinctive pictorial story on the face of the channel codes, and the great extensive animals that are being cultivated on other planets. Signaling the other planets, what is being cultivate on that planet, for commerce, and vice versa.

Sharing great enormous amounts of that one particular dominating class of animal or insect on only one planet that needed to coexist for the circle of their lives. The planets open small holes to pass feeding insects, or seeds, for food, for the live stock to strive. Making planet hunger obsolete.

They discovered that cultivating one kind of animal or insect on one planet alone caused an explosion of that particular

animal. And there would never, be a
shortness of that one particular animal, on
that planet.

This in turn created the calendar
outline, showing the insects, and animals on
the calendar, showing which planet alignment
to go to, if one desired that one particular
creature or creatures be transmitted, to
their solar system planet. Even Hell, and
Heaven, if you are capable, of channeling
with the right key.

As planet Mars had cultivating
humans, as children were instructed, and
bread to be willing slaves. The confusion of
reading the calendar without the written
text, key or instruction manual, is
impossible.

As most of the written text was destroyed when the invasion of the Spanlizards burned all the instruction manuals, on how to complete the advanced transportation units. The invaders' greed thought the natives, to be a stupid bunch of people, that had false Gods. But their true God was Israel's God. From an undiscovered buried chapter from the book of siblings. Israel's faithful large brotherhood descendants still live to this day, and God is true of giving choices of right and wrong. Humans execute right or wrong, and their own outcome prosecutes. "

As Michael smiles, and says.

"With the Trillionths, world life saving technological equipment, on the planet working, life would be different for humans. The portal would induce the Moon, and space travel to other planets, and beyond, would once again be possible.

Opening portals on other planets to doorways all over the universe, and the unknown enlightenment's.

Unfortunately, it also would open horrific dimensions yet to be discovered, and was ordered to never be opened. Allowing demons, and doorways, to what some would call the home of the Devil himself.

But some of the present occupants on the Moon, are still very familiar, with the ancient advanced builders from the past. Especially, since the evil trespassers destroyed those scriptures, scrolls, burning, and melting the replicated golden

tablets for lousy coins. What a foolish
mistake, and waste."

Michael continues with a wicked look
on his face, as the camera man zoomed in,
and said:

" Have you ever wondered why we only
see one side of the Moon from your planet or
what is on the other side of the Moon?

Not just thinking, that it is cream
cheese. But really truly thinking, what
might be on the other side of the hidden
Moon?

I am being serious about this
information, and since the world is now
ending, for most of the planets population.

Or whoever, is not in a protective bunker like the one we are in.

Yes, your future informant to the limited population, will become the union with the remaining survivors. We are breathing, and we will not be desolated. Your friendly staff here from frequency Sector 101 on the Moon. At least the area that has not been hit, by the asteroid fragments.

Yes, our broadcast station is above, so we will play this one out. It is not so bad up here on the Moon. I did not want to say anything about it since most of you listening are about to die or are already dead.

I just did not want you to be mad at us listening to how we are fine on the Moon, and your there on the planet. Do not be mad as you do not want to go out that way. I suggest start praying, if you are a believer.

The staff here on Sector 101, the Moon base anchor squad, is part of the few elite humans that will be saved, so we will still be able to broadcast the news to survivors from these reigns of destruction from the wrath of God.

Mother nature, and Angels dropping the cups of terrors from above to the grounds of the planet.

With Gods, promised command, from the covenants. He promised all, that all would

be permanently lost, and buried, once more.
To those that did not get a ticket to a
lunar space craft, may your bunkers hold up.

God's hand, and plan are in effect,
for terrifying the horrible tragic forces,
that are making these events to occur on
this planet right now. Fate, was written,
and is now procuring the covenants that God
promised to occur."

Michael drinks a 20-oz bottle of
water, and then a shot of Bourbon.

"Those still watching or hearing us,
I thank you. Now, listen up. What I am about
to inform you with is top classified
information, which would never, EVER be
released.

But since I am in a bunker here on the Moon, and you are or are not, and all my bosses are confirmed, dead.

Anyway!

I will share the information with those who are viewing or listening to my broadcast. I now have no shame, restriction or disciplining authority, to tell me not to tell you. So, I will tell you these incredible secrets. Horror is what is on the other side of the Moon, and what really happened in 2012.

I will tell you the truth. If you can handle it or not, does not matter. You will be dying shortly, unless the grace of God is kissing you. Let the truth be told as your lives, will not be, in vain. Well, in 12 hours we will know."

"Since the end is now here. There will be no harm in telling the public, what was, and is presently there on the Moon. If I have the energy, and time I will tell you so many other secrets that I wished to share with all the public in the past. But was ordered, to keep quite, on all, Top-secret society information.

I will try to tell you as much as I can, before most of you are demised by this awful wrath, God is inflicting on humans. I mostly want to tell you this information to let you know who to point the finger to, and to blame the greedy retarded Devilish people that caused this awful ending to happen, to the innocent people.

Or were humans really that innocent?

How? You may ask.

I will broadcast and dedicate this news information to you the ignorant greedy retarded Devilish people that did not know any better.

As in the past as Christ said:

("Father the children do not know what they do. Father, please forgive them.")

" These sins go especially, for you the ignorant greedy people that stole the pyramid artifacts, that may have saved the human race. It is too late, to return the stolen items. As the end, is near. The pinnacle golden tablets, the silver mix, with gold lining relics, that were glazed on The Great Pyramids, had a purpose. It was for a special, purpose, morons. A motherboard planet, was, never completed.

The UN repent-full, museums, and every other, ignorant, greedy retarded Devilish person, that held onto to these key elements of survival, are to blame. That information would have saved the mass human existence, to exist from the destruction that is now occurring. We know, that we are partly to blame."

==As Michael smiles, looks at his co-anchor, nods his head, and lifts his shoulders, as if to say why not. Then he, looks at his other co-anchor twice, and then back to the camera. Takes a whiskey shot and then with a wicked smile begins to say.

"Oddly enough this real prediction was well known for many Millenniums by many brotherhood inhabitants, like the Mayans, certain Europeans, ancient brothers from around the world, that had similar instructions, and predictions. Their instructions from the ancient wise brotherhood beings were simple.

Some occupants of the planet were brought through an energized hardware portal by the sun. Windowed in from the backside of the Moon, that was buried deep into a Moon crater.

The occupants were then launched on multi passenger, and single one man vessel

from the portal to this planet. Populating
the areas necessary to build the huge
powerful portal device that would bring the
leaders to this planet you are on.

The mission was simple to repopulate,
and finish the completion of the
strategically planned buildings on the
planet. From other highly advanced colonies,
with gear, and equipment that were far more
advance, and quicker then any digital block,
on your data co-responders.

After the population grew large
enough the ancient ones would return, and
then place more of the peaceful, brother's
families, on other planets for the families
to keep populating the galaxies. As God had,
promised the Angel decedents. All the
participating past habitant s knew, and

marked their calendars for the return, and extraction to be placed on the other galaxies.

Their missions were to build, populate, maintain, and keep the strategically placed pillars, pyramids, stoned replicated premeditated marked circles that were made of special certain materials in locations that would make large mass, space portal traveling possible, for nations.

All was possible to work as long as all the hardware devices were functional, and in place. As their construction of getting the planet ready for the Transmissions of Transportation. Otherwise, known as, (T.O.T.).

It is similar to a coded channel sound of static you may have heard on your radios, loud, and sharp.

The long sought carefully planned ancient plans were ruined by 600 fighting violent trespassing raider pioneers, demon communities. From a group called the Demon Viking Neanderthals. As the Raiders, traveled in a found wooden ship similar to Noah's wooden ship.

These medieval characters were already in war on their own planet and saw an opportunity to attack the mother ship while the space, traveling, tourists were out of their ships, from a tour in the region. As the unwanted trespassing travelers accidentally shifted the tour to the Netherlands planet, right when they were battling for territories, within their own planet.

The barbarians stumbled on a visit from a visiting tour mother ship of high-ranking families, and priests that were touring other planets.

This tour is called Planet Flash Tours, and hold up to a Max capacity of 10,000 people per trip. Tourists were aloud to view, and migrate on these planets. For scientific studies, each planet A tour ship would leave a man, and a woman on their own deserted planet. Then cultivating their own world with Gods teachings. Even the Devil's DNA traveled in the blood, and tempted the current worlds. Some planets failed.

The mistake of the pilots being,
really drunk, and failed to secure the ship
from all entry ways, from all the wine they
were drinking, was a big error. The tour
ship, planned on staying on the planet for
two weeks to see these planets, failed
developments. Before they realized the
trespassers found a portal fit, and were on
the ship. The pilots failed to take off
before being boarded by these violent
savages. The savage's plan was to steal some
of the space rocket shuttles, and travel
through wherever these tribe leaders were
going through. The raiders started
overriding the driving auto system, and
messed up the coordinates to accidentally
crash on the planet you reside on.

Some of the invaders took it off the
autopilot when they were pressing buttons.

As the auto pilot was programmed to land the shuttles safely, but since they kept pushing buttons they accidentally took it off of auto pilot. Then they placed new coordinates back to the autopilot computers, and messed the landing destinations for many of the shuttles.

The mother ships, main computer, was tampered with, and caused most of the crew ships to go off of the autopilot, when it was, suppose to land. Many died.

The wrong settings caused many accidents that killed all the high priests that had the knowledge of how to operate, and create the portals that worked. These high priests had the knowledge of the ancient ones' plans of the galaxy expansions.

The raiders traveled through the
Moons black hole portal, and without the
invitation of the high priests made a grave
error for 300 of the raiders.

That day the raiders got through
killing all the knowledge from their current
administrative leaders, architects, foreman,
builders, and all achieved humans that would
have procured the plan of finishing the
final pillars, and pyramid connection system
for the planet. All the Mayan tribal leaders
got killed from the space shuttles crashing
through, and into the buildings where all of
the leaders would normally congregate having
the great national annual conference of
peace.

All the relevant, main important leaders from around the world, were present that day. They, were all celebrating about the progress for the creation of how close they were to finishing the pillar pyramid portal system.

All the high priests gathered that day as a celebration of some of the last induction al connections, and erections of Great Pyramids. This would finalize the firewall for the planet. A remarkable shield overlaying the planet, and allowance for large land parcels or even three large countries could be transported, at an instance.

The completion of the final security systems on the planet had been severed by the raiders, and shorted down the infrastructure. This effect was making a breach on the pyramid paralleled, security structure. This system, if completed, would have, temporarily disallowed any intrusion going in or out without the shield walls opening or closing up.

The first stolen pirated space shuttle with a transmitter injector disrupt or, made it through. It crashed fast, hard, and hit a communication tower of hydrogen tanks that destroyed half the city. This further, rendered communication to the leaders around the world while it was shortly inoperable, and then permanently from all the other crashing raiders that followed.

Destroying the cities from the transportation shuttles. The shuttles were

destructive missiles hitting grand assets,
and became missiles with live passengers
that died on impact. The recklessness of
these trespassers disrupted the bloodline to
our civilization that was 1,000 times more
advanced then any contemporary culture your
living in.

300 raiders got killed in the
invasion, and exploded on impact. A lot of
strategical city portals, and flight zones,
were destroyed. All the important people,
were getting ready to congregate, at planet
Sector 1, for the 1st meeting from this
newly acquired galaxy in the dangerous, far
cosmos.

Unfortunate, luck or destiny had it
for the universal leaders being at the wrong
places, and the wrong time. Coincidental or

fate? These actions killed all the traveling leaders in different parts of the worlds. So much human knowledge was lost that day.

Other portals that launched, the raider shuttles, were being located recklessly on the destination controls, and destroyed portals among different worlds.

Since, the space ports on this planet were not ready to accept shuttles to land in the cities. The 601st raider that tried to travel through the Moon base, not knowing the big accident that would shift the pods control gear, and destroy most of the Moon base.

This action rendered some of the portals useless, and it disallowed more demons, from the, retarded Vikal Raiders, to come through to this galaxy. The emergency auto pilot kicks in, and will only take them to the portal of the Lake of Fires.

Some of the Raiders, space shuttle coordinates, turn off the auto trip programming. Making the shuttles go through the portal, incorrectly. The shuttles, impacted the ground so hard it pierced the planets core, destroying, total population, annihilation, in many other planets, that were coordinated. They became projectiles like meteors hitting the planet.

The final main devices conducting towers were destroyed from one of the clumsy, 601st, trespassing shuttle bandit. The system is down, and not to be used again until rebuilt, with the righteous humans.

The calculations of all the drivers were way off, and no matter where they landed, they would cause destruction. One, destroyed practically the whole unit of one of the pyramids top.

Most of the children passengers on a few vessels, which crashed on the planet survived. But, some of the travelers landed on key strategical cities, wiping the main buildings, and destroying the chances of the portals to be functional again till rebuilt. Millions of years later.

Some of the rockets killed the high priests that had the plans to complete some of the buildings, rendering it impossible to make the portal work without the completion of the system.

Other rockets that landed killed many of the civilizations that were on the planet. Making it impossible for the completion of some of the Great Pyramids to function. Without the human knowledge labor, to complete the tasks.

That is why the Spaniards were welcomed to the minority ignorant Mayan communities. As the Mayans innocent and ignorant, minds of the abiding citizens thought, the visitors, were futuristic men with the shinny gear they wore. As all the knowledge was held by only the elite group.

The inexperienced raiders that took possession of the alien spacecrafts were ruthless people. They wanted to rule the people, and slowly slaughter these peaceful civilizations that were the contemporary standards before the invasion.

Their demon numbers that survived the crash landing on your planet were out numbered, but conspired to make it into a demon nation like there predicating planet takeovers. The UN-savvy raiders, did not know how to use any of the Crystal Com coders, or the ships navigation system. The raiders thought the controls were useless pretty rocks that illuminated. Not aware of the great technology in these crystal controls.

All the space shuttle rockets were destroyed by the raiders ignorance. With the primitive skills the raiders had made the advance technology into worthless paper weights. Making the system inoperable, and

would never properly, work for the
intruders.

With limited knowledge these demons
would ripple the planets destiny. For the
host's technology was becoming, and was
rendering useless for the crystal ionic
field imploded. They valued these crystals
as mere decorations, and never knew, what
the ionic power disruptor possibilities
within. All the controls looked like
sparkling stones to them.

On other planets, the raiders
presence interrupted the prime objective of
the ancient builders of the black holes. One
space rocket shuttle crashed on stone hedge
breaking the completed, airport, built
circle. The other rocket ships crashed all
around the planet.

Their, desperation for survival, and their primitive understanding of this advance peaceful civilization, hurt mankind deeply.

This information I tell you would have made, concern to present few select secret societies. Some have called them The Chosen Saints for the Elite Group. Some of the architect pyramid builders around the world, knew what I am about to tell you are true. The surviving knowledge of pyramid builders passed this information down to their generations, and the generations after them that survived the brutal murders of the ignorant greedy Devilish humans that attacked in the past.

These great wise past humanitarians, architects, and builders were killed by thieves for the treasures that were in, and on top of these great pyramids. These artifacts, and treasures were really made for the survival of the human race.

But these invading, ignorant idiots did not realize this at the time. These stolen treasures were not made for the top of fireplace mantels of these Devilish thieves that placed it in a living room or private showrooms you would, have never got invited to go see.

These treasures really became worthless pieces of metal, the day these ignorant thieves stole the artifacts. Especially worthless on the final day of the end of the world. As it is a tool for testing humanities' unity for survival.

The pyramid architect builders ordered to carve, and paint the surviving instructional information on drawings like their calendar, and other artifacts, like the golden tablets that, tell the story of salvation, and destruction.

The instructions were buried deep underground with storage, for world survival instructions. These warnings, were meant to save humanity, but did warn people like my selected elite few that will repopulate the world with me when these horrific tragedies are all over.

I can't wait to get started. Not many people have seen these great golden tablets but a select elite few souls have been allowed to actually visibly see these private golden tablets that are here, in our private bunker showroom.

Why were the Mayans attacked? And for what? Those idiots from the past that attacked the Mayans in the past looked at a small picture of greed by stealing the future of all civilizations on this planet.

The greedy invaders, and archaeologists stole a lot of artifacts, gold, silver, Crystal Skulls, crystal hard drives, and advanced technological equipment. That, has, been barely understood by a few decades ago, Giving us instructions on preparation of this day.

We still have not cracked all the information from Crystal Skull number 7. But the Crystal Skull, did warn us, of today's date. These greedy beasts had no idea that they were locking the fate of humanities destruction by stealing these precious life saving devices.

The thieves did not know how to use or read the artifacts at the time. But of course only thought of their pocket books, and of how shiny these artifacts were, or how pretty the pictures, and drawings looked on the shiny golden tablets.

Some of the invaders, and thieves that invaded these sacred grounds in Mexico, mostly wanted territory to migrate for new colonies. Instead these invaders got the land but did not know what they really had.

Part of what they did not know, that the communities were large engraved parcels, communicating to space, from this civilized peaceful colonists. The thieves did not even know they were on a real gold mine, (land with large funny drawings only visibly from outer space).

The invading thieves thought they had large ambition by taking the land, and gold. And they did not realize it mostly came from outer space. The invaders did not realize that their ignorance made them have any idea that their ambitions were, really minuets. These invaders just wanted land, and treasures, claiming it was from God. As, with God's wrath for them leading astray, and praying to false gods. God will wipe out the civilization, no matter the decree.

Not knowing, that in fact they could have taken large planets with unlimited amounts of gold, and other treasures with the powers that would have been revealed to them after a certain amount of time, and tests from the peaceful Elite colonists unlocking the doorways to a vast universe.

Instead the invaders lead astray, and also suffered punishments for leading astray. As tine went on, and allowed the covenant to continue progression. Some possessed a small southern territory that is now part of the Americanas.

The technologies, the invaders held among their grasps could have conquered worlds, but being idiots did not know the true powers these aliens hid from the invaders. The surviving colonist's information, and secrets were passed down to generations, and their generations after them. The colonists went North, and disguised themselves among their native brothers, and sisters in the Northern regions from Califas, all the way East to the coast of Mayanami, and Mayne.

As time continued more ignorant greedy colonists heard of the pseudo, free land, and fought for more land which then the Aztecs-Mayans were classified as pilgrims. Cowboys, and the disguised Indian era were the only thing that finally took the final knowledge of an advanced generation alien specious secrets to their graves.

These, so-called relative, Indians
were the last known human living proof that
lived among us, and took that knowledge of
the pyramids to their graves.

Their story of leaving this planet
and instructions of controlling the axis of
the planet was written on the missing Golden
tablets that would give the special
coordinates to build the final pyramid
control modules. To save the planet by
controlling the magnetic turbulence to
safety from any disasters in the planets
path.

The only golden tablet we hold has
only the story of these advance specious
that would coexist with planets in other
galaxies, and return here to your planet,
through a black hole after the calendar

construction finished before 2012. All the time portals of course would have to be in tact and set strategically on the planet allowing the energy, and the planets, magnetic flux to operate.

The Great Pyramid powers on the planet with the pyramids on the Moon would coincide with the alignments of the galaxies, and using the Suns nova light to bounce large data transferring ionic mass to redirect the vibrational sound to transport mega tons of cities.

The mission of these civilizations was to populate the planet peacefully with any other living intelligent beings on the planet and allow the peaceful humans to coexist and allow to explore the doors of the cosmos with the advanced alien beings, and intelligent habitants.

This amazing technology would also, be used as an emergency evacuation exit system for city relocation's, and all the inhabitants parcels would have transported through the worm hole, safely to a new planet if there was any danger on the residing planets.

This technology would save the world if the planet was ending, and would be used to control the planet to move or relocate. Being able to control, and move its great magnetic field to a safer location, and then back to its orbit if deemed safe again."

Michael loosens his tie, and drinks more water. Then takes another shot of Real

Honey Whiskey. Takes a deep breath, and continues.

"The invaders that slaughtered these peaceful habitants saw pictures on walls, and thought these beings were primitive, and drew like little kids with silly imaginations. The story on the tablets fore told a wormhole so big that it was capable of ascending or descending five billion people into the population through a black hole gate.

The gate is on the other side of the Moon hiding an unaltered Great Golden Pyramid in the mist and with the help of using all the energized Great Pyramids on the planet, while activated, and energized would open the black hole, wormhole gates. Located up above on the dark side of the

Moon. The black hole wormhole is capable of transporting its hosts in a split second to any other energized black hole wormhole throughout the universe, like lightning.

Unfortunately, this task would now be impossible, since the stolen artifacts that were on top of each pyramid on the planet throughout the world, were stolen by many different types of primitive thieves. None of the doorways could now be opened without the completed circuits of the Great Pyramids that should have been grounded on the planet. Of course using the buildings as batteries, and being energized by the Sun.

The more powerful the solar flares that the sun emitted, the longer the portal could be activated. The sun would activate, and energize the pyramids on the Moons craters, and open doorways allowing humans to pass to other safe worlds, and back.

That is why the Moon has so many transportation craters built into its very core on the Moon. The stolen artifacts were, like a missing light bulb stolen from a light bulb socket.

The circuit would not illuminate without the bulb. The switch, and electricity would be there but if the light bulb was missing, it is impossible to illuminate. A simple circuit that a child could figure out, once taught the basics of the circuit.

These pyramids working together, could open the doorway in space, and actually open several black holes at a

time. Windows of new Black holes, to new
undiscovered worlds.

This plan was made by the ancient
Angels during their Olympics, against the
Devils. This would have taken most humans
into safety to one of our sister planets.
While this planet went through its
reformation, and cooled from the rapture. In
a way there would have been many repeated
raptures from this event.

This, being fore told, and bringing
the prophecies of the Bible to be true of
the rapture, taking the naked bodies to new
worlds.

The chosen people would have traveled
to other planets safely, while the
extinction of the evil inharmonious beings

would have been extinct by being left behind on this murdering planet, just like the dinosaurs experienced on this planet.

This rapture prevention machine was the human races' method, of transporting to great wonderful planets like the Garden of Edem. Also, as written, it would have transported humans to the planet Joventude, that holds the fountain of youth in the center of a great garden. Of course the tree of knowledge has been recorded to be on the Northern side of that garden."

Michael smiles largely, and says.

"Therefore, these ancient beings would have transported us to other planets, and would have descended us to other more soothing life styles for the chosen unraptured humans. For the story goes that all the humans that were chosen would get a new body from the fountain of youth.

Us being the elite few here at Studio 711 and maybe a few survivors that are left on the planet will help us finish building the rest of the pyramids. And taking the last artifacts from the dead idiots that held them from us in the past.

Finally, being deemed, the last few survivors, we will be officially the new, Elite chosen ones. After we figure out how to crack the rest of the 7th Crystal Skull, we have here in our showroom. We will be taken into a little black hole, and be stationed on many different beautiful planets, and be given, to us, the sweet nectar of the fountain of youth, at

Joventude Planet. Giving us the new bodies
as the Bible prophesies, have, covenanted.
Forever the right of mana.

But of course the story does not
specify how the process occurred. Since the
pyramid artifacts from within, and the
exterior artifacts were also taken, and not
brought back made the travel for us
impossible. Guarded by certain armies that
will be either dead or be part of the Elite,
with us. Since, we will be one government
after the world recycles, its new birth."

Michael drinks more water, and
continues:

"The past Pyramid grave robber
invaders, which wrote about the fountain of
youth did not realize that they went through

an active doorway through a portal worm hole from a cloud being the activator, transporting the occupants into another planet by the name of (Joventude).

This planet on the other side of our universe held the fountain of youth. The most beautiful planet with the planets palette core is filled with love. The idiot invaders just walked into one of the portal stations that had accidentally opened one of the gates at the right time, and moment, but the invaders never realized they were in another world, on the other side of the universe.

The transport is instantaneous, and you wouldn't know you were on the other side of the universe by walking four feet through a lighted walkway that is lightly refreshing with a breeze of wind.

It was like walking into an air-conditioned room, after just getting out of being outside on a day of temperatures at some sizzling, 100 degrees. That is the reason why they could never find the fountain of youth ever again.

The map they drew, and wrote was correct at the portal destination. But the doorway would never be opened with the circuitry being severed.

All the artifacts, and circuitry would have to be put back to utilize this great technology. Where else do you think we got some of the advanced circuits, and advanced technology from?

The Pyramids, and the crystal hard drives of vast information that has led us to the movie eras, and of course our smart humans that took this technology, and played with it for years advancing mostly by accidents but having successful attributes in their lifetime.

Not all partitions have been able to be deciphered from these crystals but as you can see we have had a great amount of alien toy technology for our lives. However, these ignorant museums, shareholders or the black market collectors made the Pyramids a useless pile of rocks, sand, and dirt by not returning the precious artifacts.

They thought they could unlock all the keys, and have all the technology for themselves. But did not realize, without all components, assembled, they were deemed, paper weights.

The pyramid time gates, also known as black holes, are so powerful that when the pyramids were functional, and fully energized by the sun, would be capable of taking whole cities or mass populations at a blink of an eye to other planets.

When functioning the Pyramids were so powerful that it could transport cities or a state if required to its new destinations, billions of miles away."

"In 2012 our newest radar technologies, and satellite, data studies, from up in the sky have faint readings on perhaps a raider signal that have showed us our records on history, did confirm that a small time gate did appear, and open a small micro but a static doorway nano signal in the year 2012.

In my opinion the world would have not ended if the greedy thieves would have united with the united councils of my planet. The completion to rebuild, and rectify the pyramids, and coil placements in strategical locations, as to function as it did in the past records of history. Life would have, only ended, for a few thousand, rather then a few billion casualties.

There would be many humans alive except for those that God chose to brandish their souls to the other sides of life. Only a few chosen elite souls would have transported into a realm that only the

cosmos would have soon revealed to many. The
end of the world, Two thousand twelve in our
calendar year, as scientists have broken
down, has proved indefinitely way off, by
astrological alignments, have proved this to
be true.

When the Moon planet is aligned with
Alpha Megateractial or, Orion, will make the
Milky way galaxy endure the resonance of the
new planet alignments. But, like I said most
of the general public would not even know it
is happening.

When the Mayans, were invaded, the
Indian leaders ordered everyone to scatter,
and to bury, and cover all the North, and
South pyramids, and artifacts. This disguise
was so that not even a satellite eagle eye

could recognize it was a Pyramid from the
sky.

The Mayan leaders ordered a large
quantity of Indians to travel North, and
cover all the other relevant Pyramids, all
the way up to what is known, as Alaska
today.

The Northern, and Southern Pyramids
were hidden by the surviving Mayans, by
covering the Pyramids with dirt and seeding
the grounds, so that weeds, and brush would
grow on top, and not be easily seeing by
satellites or more invaders in the future.

Those hidden Pyramids, and the
underwater Pyramids are still functional to

send small frequencies, but not strong enough to energize for larger frequencies to transport cities or mass human bodies. History has shown us that there were, disturbance, and weird frequencies in the area of Cholola, around these Pyramids in 2012.

The year of 2012 had more records of lightning storms ever recorded, and we are not sure if there were any people transported to or from these great devices.

We were able to find the location of all the other Pyramids that were not raided, and we were able to seclude, and preserve the Pyramids from other invaders, so we could study these newly discovered Pyramids in 2012. The lightning storms led us to these Pyramids but to this day without unlocking the final information from Crystal Skull number 7. We are, still at, huh?

We were from the beginning of the studies, and still unable to unlock the final data from the skull. We believe the few energized pyramids were able to transport a few souls that might have illegally taken host possession by a few 100 humans in the year 2012. But scientists are unclear or 100% sure according to current scientists from the recorded images of that day in 2012. There is no evidence that these phenomenons, ever existed or if this did occur.

Rumor is that there may have been alien souls that emerged onto this planet and may have possessed, and may have been one of our great leaders or great geniuses of the past in 2012 and beyond. No one is certain if this technology really existed, but now it is too late to even try to speculate, since the world now may be at an end. It was also, said that there are two set of Pyramids in groups throughout the planet to resonate a controlled magnetism for a balanced harmonious alignment and to protect the planet from magnetic disturbance, and create a shield coming directly from the active Pyramids, and the Suns energy.

Theses Pyramids were all scattered on your planet by higher powers, not just on land but in the buried seas. The secrets that the Pyramids would have foretold, would be, enlightening, to all humanitarians for the safety of the select few that has not trembled onto evil vibrant forces that have been against humanity since day one, tricking, and inducing harm against humanity.

The Hell, it will bring, to the tormented souls, that had no faith, and were left behind without this technology that is now destroying the planet, that you are on. Affecting, all the inhabitants living on our planet. The calendar going backwards, and then forward from the lunar positions, and cosmos have concluded the correct calendar year from the Mayans to our calendar year is actually 2066 on the 6th day of the 6th month on the 6th hour.

The past calendar readings have been scientifically proven wrong, since we use a 12-month calendar year opposed to the Mayans 18-month calendar year.

This off set is equivalent to what scientist have analyzed, and have deciphered the end of the world to be the real 2012, is 2066. The readings of the calendar of 2012 were actually the arrival attempts, of these advanced beings transported to our planet.

Therefore, the two annual calendars have been off by a 6-month spread, causing a differentiated conclusion, and the years, and the discovery of the wrong calendar, day, and year, will enlighten all, since we now live past the year 2012 and the world did not end for some of us in existence.

With the recently new discovery of the Calendario Mayano, artifact in Mexico, has proven the alignments recalculations. The Calendario Mayano was a new discovery a year ago, and determines that our years have been way off. The Calendario Mayano shows the true doomsday prevention day, not the year 2012 as this year of written history, only. There were plenty of deaths on that day as they experienced the rapture, and Armageddon as some would call, as that day was their final, last day on the planet."

Michael stretches, and drinks some water, then continues.

"However, if the Great Pyramids of the worlds would have been rebuilt in time, and if we would have found the Calendario Mayano in time then we would have been able to activate the powers of these Great Pyramids, by powerful magnifying inductive transportation machines that were hidden behind the Moon. This completed the puzzle,

by connecting the aligned artifacts,
Pyramids, towers, and coils, together. This
would have allowed us to control, and move
the Moon, and the planet, from harms way.
This magnetic field of the planet, would
have allowed us to move the planet like an
advanced Mother ship, similar to sci-fi
robotic planets capable of transporting
itself, around the universe. And brought us
all to safety, with the discovery of, The
Controller of the Calendario Mayano, also
known as the Calendario Mayiticano. Since it
was released by the Spanlizard Government,
before the crash"

Camera man, Bob, says to Michael.

"You have to check out the
live streams coming in."

Michael opens up his eyes wide, and smiles, nods his head, and begins again.

"We now go live to some of the uncensored, uncut scenes around the world to show you the mass fatalities, and destruction that are going on right now. Please be warned, if you have access to stay inside a bunker or a dedicated military facility, try to stay inside, and do not leave, for any reason. For your own safety, and life depends on it."

The news streams, displays, video of Moon meteoroid rocks, blasting humans, and melting their body parts.

Lava is bursting from the planets crust and water starts flooding most cities. Videos show the lava flowing like rivers,

and engulfing a mass amount of human
casualties, burning their legs off, and then
swallowing mass casualties.

In other parts of the world, videos
show tsunamis, avalanches, of tidal waves,
and flood waters, flooding the whole
country. Lava melting, and killing, all the
population, of Africa with boiling lava, and
hot waters. The ozone layer is now non
existent.

Michael Angelo goes back on the air,
and says,

"I'm not sure what will go on in the
next few hours but I can assure you this."

All of a sudden, the Moon gets hit by
meteoroids, and shatters apart. A cluster,

of meteoroids strike, and pierce, into the space station. One melting asteroid, projectile, pierces, right through the back of Michael's head, and through the front of his mouth. The burning rock left him, with a big, see through hole, while the live video feed is still rolling.

There is silence now on the air waves from the rest of the crew, getting hit and killed by the clusters of asteroids compromising the Moon, space station. The camera is still recording, streaming, and there are now only dead bodies on the space station. Only pure silence is heard, on the air waves, and the video streams the last sounds of humanity, on this planet. The next few minutes, pure dead silence.

Then, all over the world satellites, and radio frequency signals are lost for all Television broadcasts, and radio. There is no more media broadcasting anywhere on the planet. The world is now being engulfed with layers of lava all around the world. All water on the planet is evaporating into a giant boiling cloud of gas above the Northern Hemisphere. The moldering lava destroys, and burns all objects in its path. The moldering lava eventually evaporated all the waters on the planet and engulfed, all of humanity, with Hell.

Most of the peoples bunker rooms that hid in underground caves, and bunkers notice that the air temperatures in these hidden rooms are becoming to a boil, from the layers of lava above them. The humans in the underground caves, and bunkers were now covered with miles of lava above them. There fortified fortresses are melting from the liquid lava above them and start melting into their fortified entrances. Eventually an overflow of lava forces its way into the fortified solitudes that could keep them safe from nuclear destruction, but not from an act of God, that has been covenanted for ignoring the words of salvation.

The flow of lava was like water flowing into roofs that leaked during heavy rains. Eventually the lava incinerates their fortified fortresses, killing the hidden elite few that are now equal to all humans on the planet. Dead.

All human souls vaporize into an invisible state, and are embedded into, a juicy grapevine bubble like shell. Filled

with amniotic fluid that we knew from birth.
We are wide awake frozen in time, looking
out of this grape in a grapevine filled,
with flat ovary cells. We are placed in a
time capsule, now waiting, and knowing there
are no emotions in our thoughts. No,
personal feelings, but a blank vision of
silence, and view of dirty water in our
eyes, knowing now that your dead, not
knowing what will come next. The only
feeling is similar to being hit in the head,
and starting through your first year after
birth. Not knowing anything.

The worst part is that you will never
be able to feel, flesh again. Or breathe
that soothing, rich, refreshing oxygen we
love to breathe causing the perpetual circle
we call life. Instead your wide awake, not
even resting but awake, starring deep to

other souls across from you. That look like
baby tadpoles, waiting to see what is next,
not knowing with blank looks, and blank
random, sensations for possibly eternity.
With everyone looking like little aliens, as
you looked like, when in your Mothers' womb.

This makes time, frozen, locked up in
a time, that never ends.

New souls are extracted, and
imprisoned in the Grape Vine clusters,
waiting for their turn in line, to be called
upon. Until your number is called, you will
wait forever, it seems. And that day may
never come, for some. Or, may not be called,
until, a few millenniums from now. A real
prison, but not Hell.

CHAPTER THREE

The Grapevines of souls.

The Grapevines of souls.

        Ovarian Grapevines of Hibernating

Unassigned Souls.

        One of the Truths in death.

        Now the souls of the people of the

planet, were separated, to different realms

of God's backyards. Most of the souls went to the

Grapevines of souls. The souls would be sucked out of human life, by the Soul Extractors, and sent to, The Golden Gate of Saint Peter's doors of Realms. These grapevines are like clusters of grapes, and grapevines that hold similar to a human branch like grapevines of ovary eggs. Just imagine an endless long life, of beings, being locked up in a tiny cell, for an eternity. Just like you were locked up in a tiny ovary cell. A grapevine, that holds all the souls in a cell, that is situated in the cosmos. For what might be, just an eternity, with no way out. In each grape cell bonds-

33 Crystal Skulls & The Anti+Christ

BOOK 2 OF 7

www.ingramcontent.com/pod-product-compliance
Lightning Source LLC
Chambersburg PA
CBHW020702030726
47498CB00002B/598